Editor's Note

The three stories in this book,
    The Emperor's New Clothes,
    The Three Wishes,
    and The Master of All Masters,
are delightfully nonsensical, but in each of them you will
find an element of sense if you look for it.
    The Emperor's New Clothes *was written by Hans
Christian Andersen in 1836. It is a very funny story about
the folly of a king who will not admit he has made a
mistake.* The Three Wishes, *while piling absurdity upon
absurdity, suggests it is wise to think before you speak. It
first appeared in English in Madame LePrince de
Beaumont's "The Young Misses Magazine" in 1761. The
Master of All Masters says something for plain speaking.
It is an old English folktale and was among those collected
by Joseph Jacobs in the late nineteenth century.*

THE EMPEROR'S NEW CLOTHES and Other Nonsense Stories

Illustrated by Karen Milone

A GOLDEN BOOK • NEW YORK
Western Publishing Company, Inc., Racine, Wisconsin 53404

The Emperor's New Clothes

MANY YEARS AGO there lived an Emperor who was so fond of new clothes that he spent all his money on them. He had a different coat for every hour of the day, and it was always said, "The Emperor is in his dressing room."

In the large city where he lived, visitors arrived every day. One day there came two impostors pretending to be weavers who knew the secret of weaving the most beautiful fabrics that could be imagined. Not only were the colors and designs supposed to be uncommonly beautiful, but the fabric was supposed to possess the wonderful quality of being invisible to anyone who was stupid.

"Clothes made of that material would be most valuable," the Emperor thought. "If I had them, I could tell the clever from the stupid. That cloth must be at once woven for me." So he gave the order to the two impostors, and a large sum of money, in order that they might begin their work.

They set up two looms and set to working, but there was nothing at all on the looms. Straightaway they required the finest silk and the most beautiful gold thread to work into their cloth, which they put into their pockets, and worked away at the bare looms till late at night.

"I should like to know how they have got on with the cloth," the Emperor thought. But at the same time he was greatly embarrassed when he thought of it, for anyone who was stupid could not see it. Now, he had no doubts about himself, but he thought it as well first to send someone else, to see how it was getting on. Everyone in the city knew the special quality of the fabric, and everyone was anxious to see how stupid his neighbor was.

"I will send my old, honest minister to the weavers," the Emperor thought. "He will be best able to judge how the fabric succeeds, for he has sense."

So the good old minister went to the room where the two impostors were working at their bare looms. "Heaven preserve me!" the old minister thought, and he opened his eyes wide. "Why, I cannot see anything." But that he did not say.

Both impostors begged him to step nearer, and they asked whether he did not think the design pretty and the colors beautiful. They then pointed to the bare loom, and the poor old minister opened his eyes still wider. "Can it be possible," he thought, "that I am stupid? That I would never have believed, and no one must know it. It will never do to tell that I cannot see the stuff!"

"Well, you say nothing of our work," one of the weavers said.

"Oh, it is very pretty! Quite beautiful!" the old minister said, looking through his spectacles. "The design and the colors—yes, I shall not fail to tell the Emperor that it pleases me very much."

"We are delighted to hear it," both the weavers said, and then they mentioned all the different colors, and explained the unusual design. The old minister paid great attention, that he might use the same words when he returned to the Emperor. And he did so.

The impostors now applied for more money, more silk, and more gold, to be used in their weaving, which they put in their pockets, for not a single thread was put upon the looms, though they continued their pretended work.

The Emperor soon after sent another statesman to see
how the weaving got on and whether the cloth would soon
be ready. With him it was exactly as with the other. He
looked and looked, but as there was nothing besides the
bare loom, he could see nothing.

"Well, is that not beautiful cloth!" the two impostors
asked, and then explained the magnificent design which did
not exist.

"I am not stupid," the man thought, "and I must never let
it be suspected." So he praised the fabric which he did
not see, and assured them he was highly pleased with the
beautiful design and colors. "Oh, it is lovely," he said to the
Emperor.

Everyone in the city spoke of the magnificent fabric.

The Emperor now wanted to see it himself, so with a host of followers, he went to the two artful impostors, who now worked away with all their might, though without a thread.

"Is it not magnificent?" the two impostors asked. "Will not Your Majesty look more closely and examine the design and beautiful colors?" And they pointed to the bare loom.

"How is this?" the Emperor thought. "Why, I see nothing at all. It is quite dreadful. Can it be that I am stupid? That would be the most dreadful thing that could happen."

"Yes, it is very beautiful!" he said. "It has my highest approval." And he nodded with apparent satisfaction at the bare loom, for he would not admit that he did not see anything.

All his followers looked and looked, seeing no more than
the others, but they said the same as the Emperor, and they
advised him to wear clothes of that magnificent fabric at the
approaching grand procession. "It is delightful, charming,
excellent!" passed from mouth to mouth, and all seemed
really delighted. The Emperor awarded both the impostors
medals to wear in their buttonholes, and dubbed them
Court Weavers.

The whole night before the procession was to take place, the impostors were up, and had more than twenty lights burning. Everyone could see that they were very busy getting the Emperor's new clothes ready. They pretended they were taking the cloth off the loom, cut away in the air with large shears, and sewed with needles without thread, and said at length, "See, now the clothes are ready."

The Emperor himself came, and both impostors raised an arm, exactly as if they were holding something up, and said, "These are the trousers, this is the coat, here is the cloak," and so on, "all so light that one might think one had nothing on. But that is the beauty of the material. If Your Imperial Majesty will please take off your clothes," the impostors said, "we will put the new ones on for you here, before the mirror."

The Emperor took off all his clothes, and the impostors pretended to help him on with one article after another of the new garments. The Emperor bent and turned about before the mirror.

"Oh, how becoming they are! How beautifully they fit!" he said. "The pattern and colors are perfect. This is a magnificent outfit!"

The castle porter came in and said, "The canopy, which is to be carried over Your Majesty in the procession, is waiting outside."

"Well, I am ready," the Emperor said. "Do not the clothes fit well?" And then he turned again to the mirror, for he wished to appear as if he were examining his attire carefully.

The pages, who were to carry the train, stooped and pretended to lay hold of something on the ground, as if they were raising the train, which they then pretended to hold up, for they would not have it appear that they could not see anything.

So the Emperor walked in the procession, under the magnificent canopy. All the people in the street and in the windows said, "The Emperor's clothes are not to be equaled. And what a magnificent train he has!" No one would let it appear that he did not see anything, for if so, he would have been thought very stupid. No clothes of the Emperor's had ever had so much success as these.

"But he has nothing on," said at length a little child.

"Good heavens! Listen to the innocent thing's voice!" its father said. And one whispered to the other what the child had uttered.

"But he has nothing on!" all the people cried at last.

It appeared to the Emperor that they were right. But he said to himself, "Now that I have begun it, I must go on with the procession." And the pages continued to carry the train which did not exist.

The Three Wishes

THERE WAS ONCE a man, not very rich, who had a pretty woman for his wife. One winter's evening, as they sat by their fire, they talked of the happiness of their neighbors, who were richer than they.

"If it were in my power to have what I wish," said the wife, "I should soon be happier than anyone."

"So should I," said the husband. "I wish we had fairies now, and that one of them was kind enough to grant me what I should ask."

At that instant, a very beautiful Lady appeared and said, "I am a fairy, and I promise to grant you the first three things you shall wish for. But take care, after three wishes, I will not grant anything more."

The fairy disappeared, and the man and his wife talked
it over.

"If it is left to me," said the wife, "I know what I shall
wish for. I do not wish yet, but I think nothing is so good as
to be handsome, rich, and of great quality."

But the husband answered, "With all these things one
may be sick, fretful, and one may die young. It would be
much wiser to wish for health, cheerfulness, and a long life."

"But what good is a long life with poverty?" asked the
wife. "It would only prolong misery. In truth, the fairy
should have granted us a dozen wishes, for there's at least a
dozen things I want."

"That's true," said the husband, "but let us take time and consider from now until morning which three things we want most, and then wish."

"I'll think all night," said the wife. "Meanwhile let us warm ourselves, for it is very cold."

At the same time, the wife took the poker and stirred up the fire. Without thinking, she said, "Here's a nice fire. I wish we had a good sausage for our supper. I could cook it up in a minute."

The words were hardly out of her mouth, when an enormous sausage tumbled down through the chimney.

"Plague on greedy-guts, with her sausage!" said the husband. "There's a fine wish indeed! Now we only have two left. For my part, I am so angry, that I wish the sausage would stick fast to the tip of your nose!"

At this second wish, the sausage leaped up and stuck fast to the tip of his poor wife's nose. Try as she might, she could not get it off.

"Wretch that I am!" cried she. "You are a wicked man for wishing the sausage to stick fast to my nose!"

"My dear," answered her husband, "I vow I did not mean it. But what shall we do now? I think we should wish for great riches. Then we could have a gold case made to hide the sausage."

"Not at all!" answered the wife. "I will not live with this sausage dangling from my nose. We still have one wish left. Leave it to me, or I shall kill myself!"

"Wait, my dear wife! I will give you leave to wish for whatever you want."

"Well," said his wife, "my wish is that this sausage may drop off my nose."

At that instant, the sausage dropped off.

The wife said to her husband, "Perhaps it is best we did not have more than three wishes. We might have been more unhappy with riches than we are now. Let us stay as we are and take things as they come. Meanwhile, we can sup upon our sausage, since that's all we have left of the wishes."

The husband agreed with his wife. They supped merrily, and never gave themselves further trouble about the things they had meant to wish for.

The Master of All Masters

A GIRL ONCE hired herself for a servant to an old
gentleman. As soon as she came to his house ready for
work, he said, "Before you begin, I want to give you some
instructions."

"Very well, sir," said she.

"In my house I have my own special names for things," he
continued, "and I want you to carefully heed and remember
what I say."

"Oh, certainly, sir. I will do that," she replied.

"Now, first," said he, "what will you call me?"
"Oh, I will call you master, or mister, or whatever you
please, sir," said she.

"No, no," said he, "you must call me 'master of all masters.' And what would you call this?" he asked, pointing to his bed.

"Oh, I would call it a bed, or a couch, or whatever you please, sir," she replied.

"No," said he, "that's my 'barnacle.' And what do you call these?" he inquired, pointing to his trousers.

"Oh, I call them breeches, or trousers, or whatever you please, sir," said she.

"You must call them 'squibs and crackers,'" said he. "And what would you call her?" he asked, pointing to the cat.

"Oh, I would call her cat, or pussy, or whatever you please, sir," said she.

"You must call her 'white-faced simminy,'" said he. "And what do you call this?" he asked, waving his hand toward the fire.

"Oh, I call it fire, or flame, or whatever you please, sir," said she.

"You must call it 'hot cockalorum,'" said he. "And what do you call this?" he asked, pointing to some water.

"Oh, I call it water, or wet, or whatever you please, sir," she replied.

"No," said he, "'pondybus' is its name here. And what do you call the building in which I live?"

"Oh, I call it house, or cottage, or whatever you please, sir," said she.

"You must call it 'high-topper mountain,'" he ordered.

That very night the servant awoke her master from a sound sleep by pounding with her fists on his door and shouting in great fright, "Master of all masters, get out of your barnacle and put on your squibs and crackers, for white-faced simminy has got a spark of hot cockalorum on her tail, and unless you get some pondybus, the high-topper mountain will be all on hot cockalorum!"

The servant remembered to use just the words her master had ordered, but was so long explaining what was the matter that by the time she finished, the house was on fire. The flames spread rapidly, and though the master and his servant escaped, the building burned to the ground.

The old gentlemen built another house, but this time he let his servant call things by their ordinary names instead of his own special ones.